For: Coral, Gramie, Grmie, Gera[...]
GoomGoom (Ainsa). I love you thanks for being awesome! Keep up the GREAT work
xoxoxoxoxoxoxoxoxoxoxo xo xoxoxo, Kate

For all children with upper limb differences

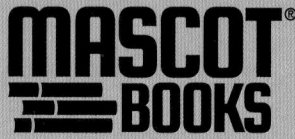

www.mascotbooks.com

Look What Kate Can Do: One Hand Works as Well as Two

©2018 Katie and Paul Leatherwood. All Rights Reserved. No part of this publication may be reproduced, stored in a retrieval system or transmitted in any form by any means electronic, mechanical, or photocopying, recording or otherwise without the permission of the author.

For more information, please contact:
Mascot Books
620 Herndon Parkway #320
Herndon, VA 20170
info@mascotbooks.com

Library of Congress Control Number: 2017913672

CPSIA Code: PRT1217A
ISBN-13: 978-1-63177-171-2

Printed in the United States

Look What Kate Can Do

One Hand Works as Well as Two

By Katie & Paul
Leatherwood

"Look what Kate can do!" says Daddy.
"This girl can do anything!" says Mommy.
It's true. I can do everything a seven-year-old can do, only in a little different way. My name is Kate, and I was born with one hand.

    I have a whole left wrist and a soft palm which is very useful, like a hand with no fingers. We call it my wrist, and it's sensitive, more sensitive than the fingers on my right hand.

    Yes, I have five fingers and ten toes, but that does not add up to me. Mommy and Daddy say I can do anything I set my mind to. My wrist and right hand work as well as two.

My parents heard lots of stories about one-handed people when I was little.

Jim Abbott, born without a right hand, became a Major League Baseball pitcher.

Tony Memmel is a singer and songwriter.

Nicole Kelly became Miss Iowa 2013.

Maureen Beck is a gold medalist paraclimber from Colorado.

"People meant well," says Mommy, "but Kate won't miss a hand she never had. It will only hurt when someone makes fun of her."

Mommy and Daddy had dreams for me, their first baby. I would walk and talk, learn to read and write my name. Now I can ride a bike and swim.

I can button my own buttons. I can open a jar. I'm learning how to type on a keyboard. When I'm sixteen, I will drive a car.

One day I might draw like Paups, my grandfather, or dance like my Aunt Kat. Mommy and Daddy say I can do anything I want to do because I have learned one hand and my wrist work as well as two. And everything I want to try, I figure out how to do.

As I walked into school one day, I heard a boy say, "Mom! That's the girl with one hand."

"You know, I can hear you," I said over my shoulder. Just because I have one hand doesn't mean I can't hear. Just because I have one hand doesn't mean I'm not smart.

My kindergarten teacher said, "It's hard to keep up with the Kate Kooglers of this world."

Types of Symbrachydactyly

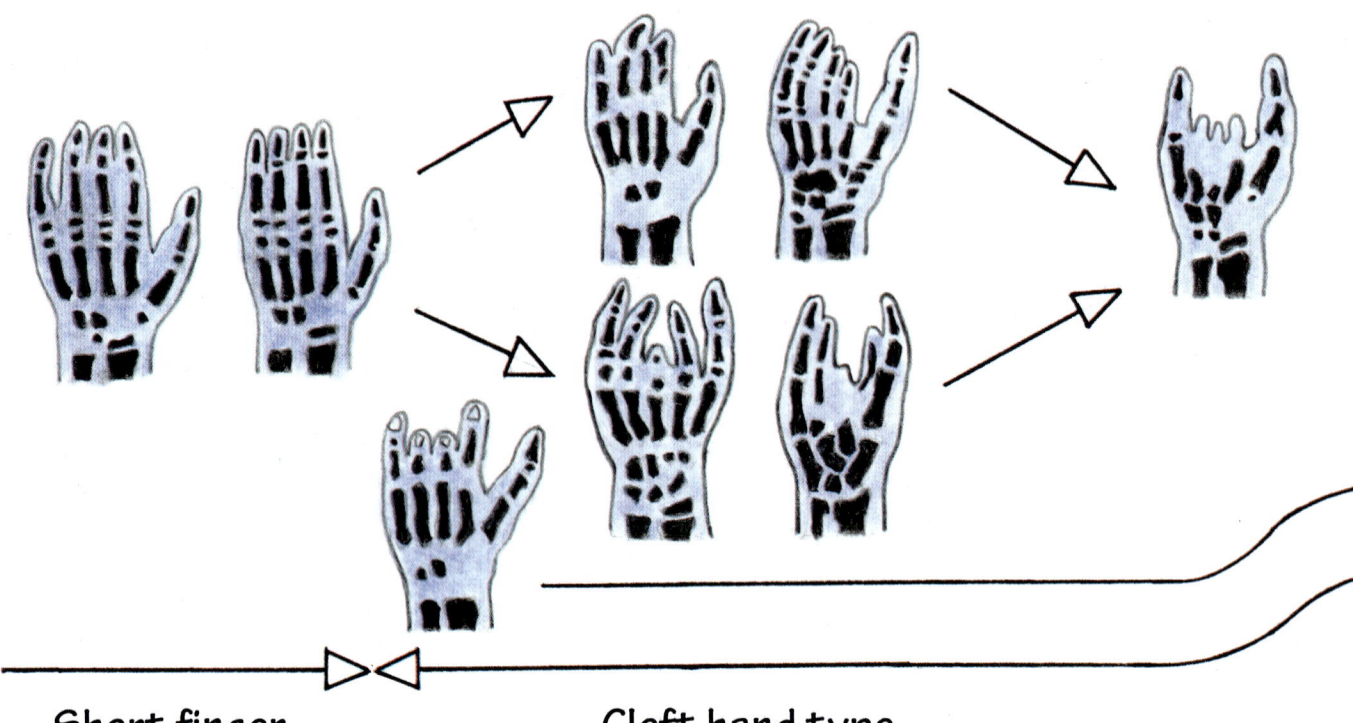

Short finger   Cleft hand type

    When kids ask me, "What happened to your hand?" I say, "I was born this way." That's usually enough.

    When Mommy was pregnant with me, my left hand stopped growing but not because of something Mommy did. Doctors don't know why some babies' hands and arms don't grow. Mommy and Daddy saw the ultrasound before I was born and knew their baby had only one hand. They prayed for healing, but I was born this way. This is how God made me. My wrist is not a mistake.

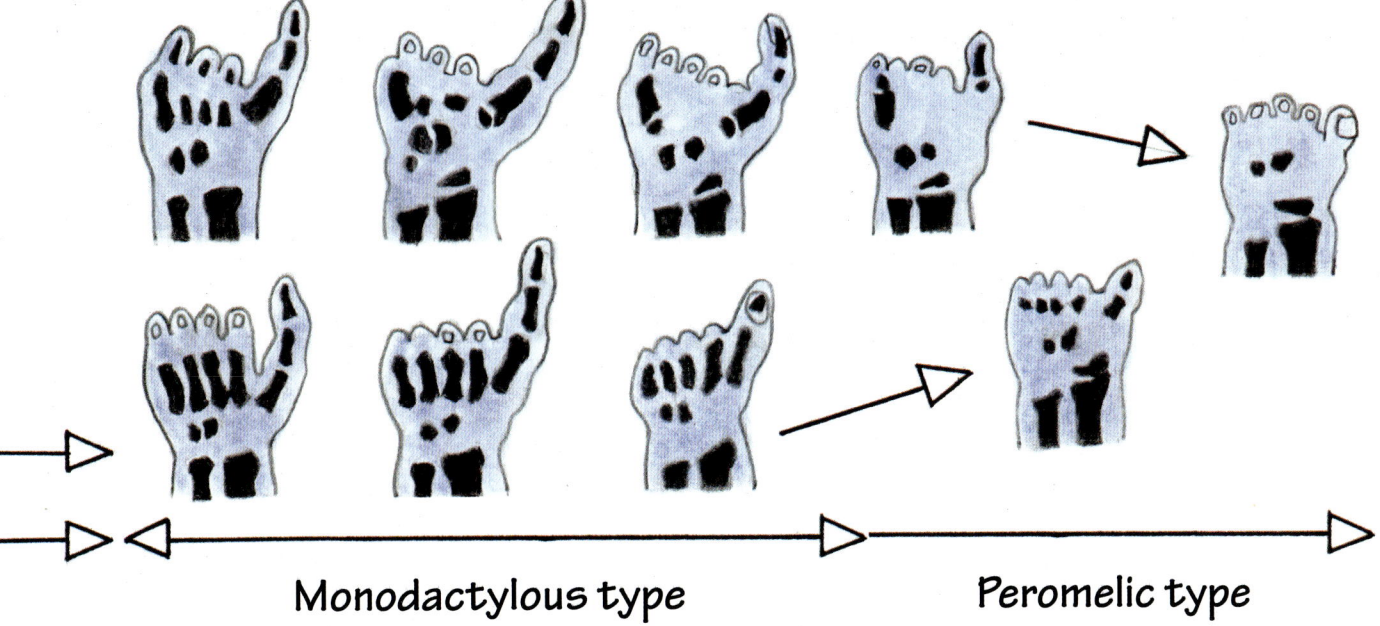

Monodactylous type   Peromelic type

Symbrachydactyly is the big word for my condition. It means I have upper limb and finger differences.

I was born with five tiny nubbins that had no bones and were very delicate. Doctors recommended surgery to remove the nubbins or I might need emergency surgery later on. My nubbins could get caught in small spaces or be hurt when I learned to crawl.

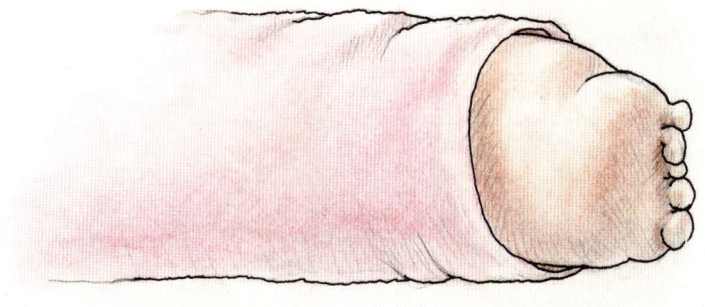

Mommy and Daddy weren't sure what to do and prayed for an answer. Then Texas Scottish Rite Hospital for Children in Dallas called with an unexpected appointment. I had surgery when I was ten months old. Mommy covered my cast with a pink sock.

Some children keep their nubbins and others have surgery to replace a finger with toe bones. Some children get prosthetics. There are many forms of symbrachydactyly and many decisions to make. Every family gets to choose what is right for their child.

Most people are curious about my wrist. Some kids are worried. They wonder if I lost my hand in an accident or if my wrist hurts. It doesn't. Some kids are afraid. They think if they get close to me, the same thing could happen to them. My wrist is not contagious. Sometimes they stare at me and want to know more.

One boy at school kept asking me, "What happened to your hand?" I answered him three times. "I was born this way." I tried to be polite but the fourth and fifth time he asked, I just ignored him. I thought, *Do you want a different answer? Like a shark bit it off? Or a bear got hold of me?*

It's hard to be different. Sometimes I wish I had two hands. I talk to Mommy and Daddy about how I feel and what kids say. They say I have three choices:

I can answer politely.

> Can I see that? What happened to your hand?

> I was born this way.

I can ignore their questions.

> Hey, what happened to your hand?

If someone is rude, I can ask them a question.

Hey, little girl! What happened to your hand?

Nothing! What happened to your manners?

I almost always answer politely, but I get tired of being bugged. I think, *Oh please, just leave me alone.*

When I'm around new kids, it's hard to have one hand. I told my mom that sometimes I feel like hiding my wrist. Mommy understands. Daddy says sometimes people don't even notice. That's true, too. After I get to know people, I feel more comfortable.

Sometimes I have to be brave. When I dance on stage, I hold my wrist up high for everyone to see. My Nana says I am a beautiful ballerina.

When I was little, I started to figure things out for myself. I learned to tie my shoes with two colors of long laces.

I have a bony point on my wrist where a thumb started to grow. It's strong and useful.

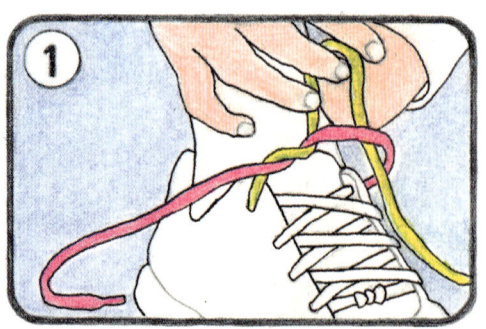

Cross the laces and loop one on the edge of my wrist.

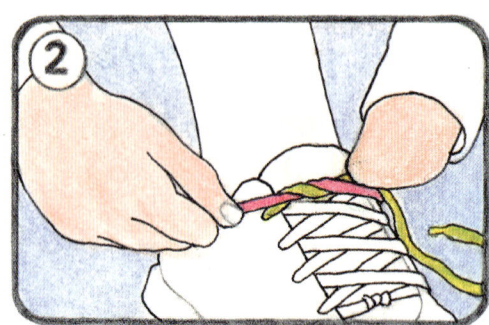

Hold the lace with my wrist and pull it tight.

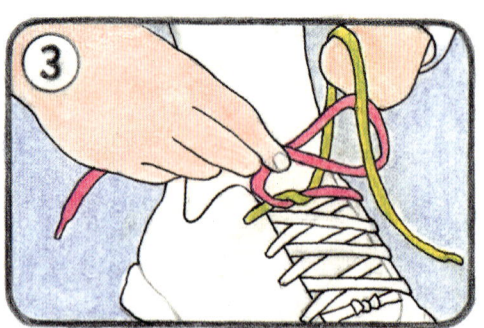

Make a loop on the left and bring the other lace around.

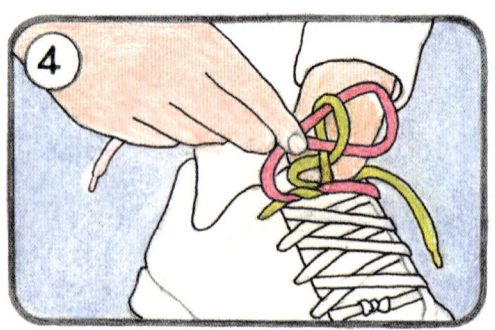

Push the loop from the back.

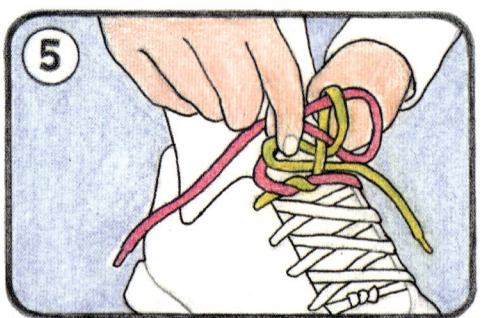

Pinch the loop and bring it through.

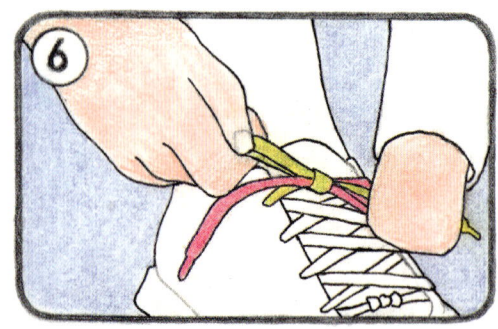

Pull the loops tight. Voilà!

    One of the most important lessons I have learned is to stand up for myself. One day a kid said, "You can't tie your shoes."

    "Yes, I can," I told him.

    "No, you can't," he said. "Your mom did that."

    My friend untied her shoe and said, "Show him, Kate," but I didn't really need to. My friend and I already knew that I could tie my shoe. We just walked away.

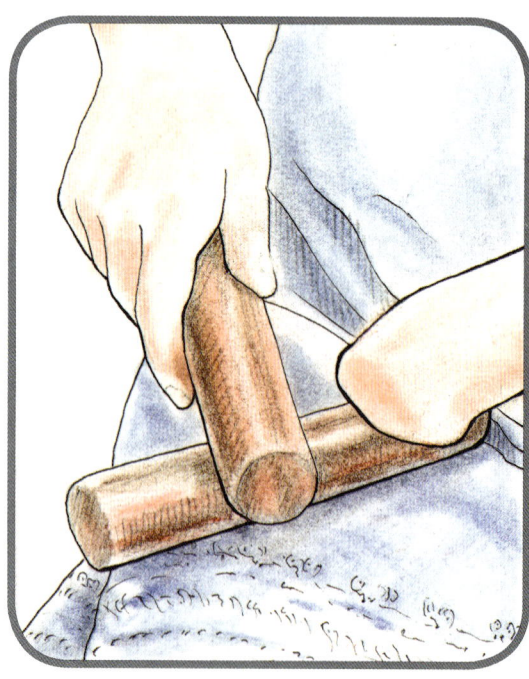 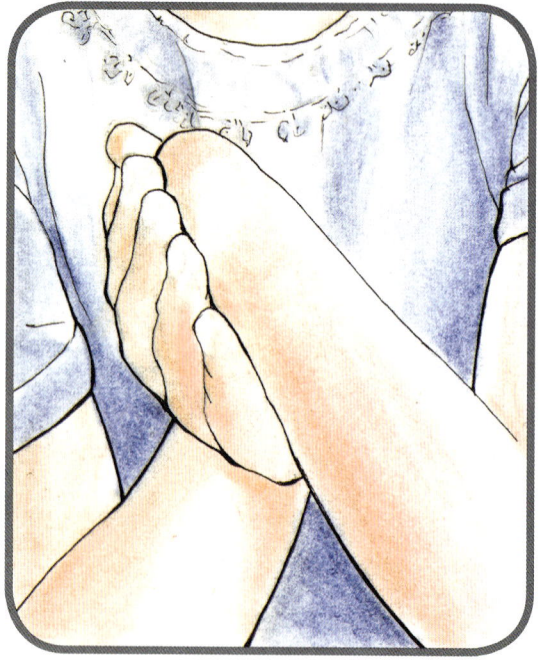

I figured out how to use a knife and fork by myself. I like to cook and help in the kitchen. On Saturdays, I make pancakes for my family.

My music teacher handed me rhythm sticks one day. I held one on my leg with my wrist and hit it with the other stick. I can clap, too. Loud!

Playing a guitar looked like fun, so Paups gave me a few lessons. Daddy made a bracelet that holds a pick so I can strum with my wrist. Like everyone else, sometimes I try something new and find out I don't like it that much. Guitar is one of those.

My PE teacher, Mrs. Shaw, has a son with one hand. She gave me the things he used in elementary school, like a cushiony block for push-ups and a velcro bracelet for jumping rope.

"Look what Sam can do!" we say. I have a friend named Sam who was born without a forearm. He can swing across the rings.

Symbrachydactyly is pretty common and happens more often than people think.

What else can I do, you ask?

I practiced braiding my doll's long hair, and I'm learning how to braid my own.

I love to polish my toenails. One day I said, "Mommy, I want to paint my fingernails."

She gave her usual answer. "You'll figure it out, Kate." And I did. I hold the brush still on my knee and move my right hand.

What else will I do?
 I want to be a mommy, a teacher, maybe even an actor someday.
 You see, my wrist and one hand work as well as two. My name is Kate Koogler, and there isn't anything I can't do.

Katie and Paul Leatherwood, also known as Nana and Paups, are Kate Koogler's grandparents. Now retired, Katie was an English teacher, while Paul taught art, illustration, graphics, and photography in Bend, Oregon. Inspired by their granddaughter's learning experiences, they have combined their talents in this children's book.